First published in Great Britain in 2020
Copyright © Victor Publishing 2020

www.victorpublishing.co.uk

ISBN: 9798575420958

The children were in the playground, Lizzie sat on her own,
She longed to join in the fun, but she sat all alone.

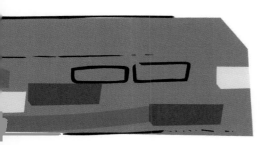

She was watching the other kids, kicking a ball,
Lizzie felt very lonely, just sitting on the wall.

She began to daydream of the
things that she liked,
Like climbing and running and
riding her bike.

But mostly she thought about how much she'd enjoy,
kicking a ball with the girls and the boys.

At home after school, Lizzie played with a ball,
Kicking it hard, against the garden wall.

"Can I join in?" said dad
as he walked out in the sun,
"Playing football together can be so much fun".

The pair played football, until mum called them in,
"It's time to eat", she called with a grin.

Both Lizzie and her dad
were in a very happy mood.
They were both so hungry,
they wolfed down their food.

Each night after school, Lizzie played football alone.
Her dad would join her, once he had come home.

One night as Dad was tucking Lizzie up in her bed.
"Can we always play football together?"
the little girl said.

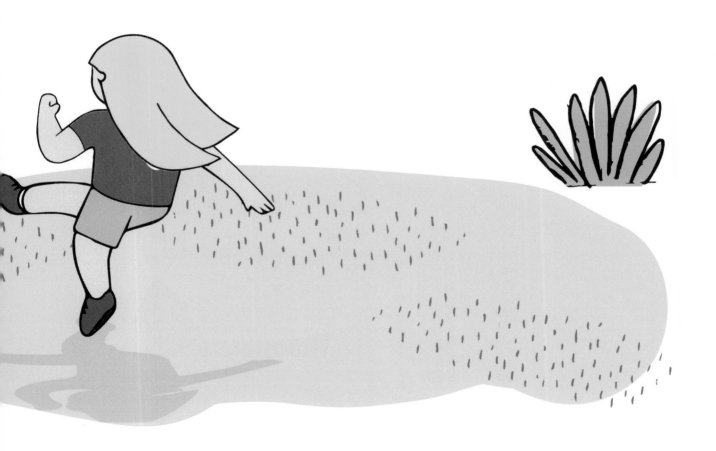

Dad knew how much his girl loved the beautiful game,
And helping her become better, was his personal aim.

That weekend, in the garden,
Lizzie couldn't believe her eyes,
Dad had built two football nets,
what a lovely surprise!

Soon Lizzie was enjoying the game, so much more.
She learned to dribble and pass, and how to score.

One day the two were joined by Lizzie's cousin Zach.
Who had arrived with his mum for a lunchtime snack.

Zach said, "I love football too,
I can play in net?".
The three played together,
it was Lizzie's best day yet.

The garden soon became the talk of her friends.
Soon there were enough players for a team at both ends.

Dad would referee, mum brought drinks at half-time.
Orange juice, blackcurrant juice and lemon & lime.

Lizzie's skills were improving with every day.
She even dreamt of football, she was so excited to play.

Her dreams were of goals,
scored with shots on the run.
Every dream made her happy,
every game had been won.

Asleep or awake, Lizzie loved her football.
All she could think of, was kicking a ball.

Football in the playground,
football in the park.
Football in the daytime,
football 'til it was dark.

Football before breakfast,
football before bed.
Dreaming of goals scored,
with her feet and her head.

With her confidence high, Lizzie was now never alone.
No more sitting on the school wall, all on her own.

She joined in the games in the playground,
enjoying the fun.
Some games were lost, and some games were won.

Thanks to her dad, Lizzie had learned how to play.
And now she played football, every day!

Football made Lizzie happy, she was no longer sad.
Football with her friends, or in the garden with Dad.

Lizzie still went running and climbing,
and riding her bike,
but they were no longer the best things she liked.

The number one thing she loves doing best,
Lizzie loves playing football, above all of the rest!

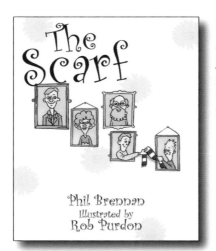

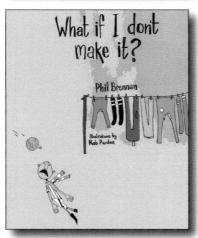

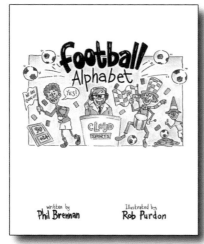

Printed in Great Britain
by Amazon

79569994R00020